Coyote Christmas

A Lakota Story

Coyote Christmas

A Lakota Story

S. D. Nelson

ABRAMS BOOKS FOR YOUNG READERS

NEW YORK

Coyote did not know that it was Christmas Eve. He only cared that his empty stomach was growling and that the shivering cold of night was settling upon the land. As he trotted along a hilltop of the Indian reservation, his ears perked to the sound of turning tires and moving metal. Below him an old pickup truck was making its way along a dirt road toward a little ranch house.

Sister Raven swooped down from the darkening sky with outstretched wings. She circled once above Coyote and perched nearby on a twisted branch.

"Coyote, you old devil, what tricks are you plotting?" asked Sister Raven.

Coyote chuckled. He did not mind being mocked by the black bird. After all, he was proud to be called the Trickster.

"Well, my feathered friend," answered Coyote, "if you hang around, I will show you. I think I'll pay those two-legged creatures a visit and get me a free hot meal."

Down the hill the Trickster went with Sister Raven tagging along overhead. He sneaked around to the side of the house. A gray-haired woman removed a pumpkin pie from the oven. Coyote smacked his lips. The one thing he admired about the two-leggeds was their food. It was delicious! Other than that, he thought people were foolish and easily duped.

A girl busily stacked pretty packages tied with ribbons. The Trickster saw a juniper tree sparkling with lights, which appeared to be growing inside the house. Coyote had heard about Christmas trees and realized it must be Christmas Eve. A boy and the girl sang a silly song about a reindeer with a red nose. Coyote listened to the entire tune, and near the end he was humming right along.

Old Coyote's empty belly groaned. That gave him an idea for a trick. He had heard stories about a man in a red suit who visits children on Christmas Eve. If he could pretend to be Santa Claus, he just might be able to get a free meal. But where, on such a snowy night, could he find a Santa costume?

The prankster decided to snoop around in the barn, but got a big surprise as he passed the corner of the house. The family's pet dog charged from the shadows under the front porch, barking, "Roo, woo, woo!"

Coyote turned, raised his paw, and declared, "Stop,
you stupid dog, or I will turn you into a house cat!" The dog
stopped dead in his tracks. He clamped his mouth shut, lowered his head,
tucked his tail between his legs, and returned to his bed under the porch.
The last thing Brother Dog wanted was to be turned into a silly cat.

Two horses and a milking cow stood in their separate pens chewing hay. Upon seeing Old Man Coyote, the startled horses stomped their hooves and cried out, "Hay-nee, hay-nee!"

"Be quiet!" demanded the Trickster. "Or I will turn you into pigs!" The horses shut up immediately. They did not want to be pigs.

The frightened cow, on the other hand, could not stop her mooing. Coyote walked right over to her wooden stall. He raised his paw and said, "Moo Cow, Moo Cow, moo no more. An owl you will be—fly out the door." In the next moment, the inside of the cow's pen became a bedlam of flapping wings. A spooked owl banged into the wall, then flew out the door into the night.

Rummaging about in the dimness, Coyote saw a faded horse blanket draped over a rail. It had a hole worn right in its middle. "Aha, this will work nicely," said the shifty character. He pulled the blanket over himself, poking his head through the hole. For a belt he tied a rope around his belly. Next, he tied a rag on his head. Turning about in a circle he chanted, "Rags I wear from foot to head, but I don't care—I'll turn them red." And in a puff of smoke, he was dressed in a red suit.

Coyote then found a fuzzy sheepskin hanging on a nail. The troublemaker tied a piece of it beneath his chin for a beard. In the corner he found an empty cloth sack, which he stuffed full of straw and slung over his shoulder. The rascal stood proudly and snickered to himself. The horses stared in silent astonishment—Coyote had been transformed into the very likeness of Santa Claus!

The Trickster walked directly toward the house and his waiting Christmas dinner. He passed the trembling dog beneath the steps and firmly pounded on the door. The music inside stopped. Grandma blurted, "Who can that be on this Christmas Eve?"

It seemed strange to her that their dog had not barked a warning as he usually did when visitors arrived.

The girl, Isabel, opened the door. There stood the fake Santa, smiling boldly. "Ho-ho-ho!" he declared. Isabel squealed with joy, "It's Santa Claus!" She rushed forward and threw her arms around the sly night visitor. The boy, Davy, sat speechless. Likewise, Grandma and Grandpa were surprised beyond words. Isabel grabbed Santa by his paw and led him into the house.

Dropping the big bag from his shoulder, Coyote said, "I have Christmas gifts for everyone." He followed that with another "Ho-ho-ho!" Isabel twirled about and asked, "Grandma, can Santa stay for dinner?"

"Bless you, my girl. You certainly have the Christmas spirit," said the fake Santa.

Grandma and Grandpa were getting old, and their eyesight was not the best. All they saw was a short figure dressed in red.

"Grandma, please," insisted the little girl.

"Well, I suppose you're right. After all, it is Christmas Eve," replied Grandma. "A hungry stranger is always welcome at our table."

Grandpa brought another chair to the table, and Coyote plopped himself down without hesitation. He licked his teeth and smacked his lips. He could hardly wait to eat.

For the first time, Coyote saw that Davy's chair was on wheels. With his hands, the boy wheeled himself toward the table and joined the others, who seated themselves. Coyote had never seen such a chair. He said, "My boy, what a curious and wonderful toy you ride on."

Davy replied, "That's what some of the kids at school say, too. It's a wheelchair, not a toy. I ride it because my legs don't work."

"Oh," said the Trickster, not really understanding.

"It's OK, Santa. I mean, I guess it's all right," said the boy in his shy voice.

Coyote, always hungry, was quickly losing interest in this talk about chairs with wheels. He reached across the table for the bowl of meatballs. When he heard Grandpa's words—"We ask for a blessing on this holy night"—Coyote quickly released the bowl. He bowed his head, put his paws together, and pretended to pray along with the humans. Grandpa continued, "Thank you for our health and our happiness, and merry Christmas to all."

The prankster had never eaten spaghetti with meatballs before. It was Grandpa's favorite dish, so Grandma had prepared it especially for Christmas Eve dinner. At first Coyote had trouble slurping up the long, wiggly noodles. The old coot ate and ate until he had to loosen the rope around his swelling belly. When Grandma offered him a wedge of pumpkin pie, he actually hesitated. But after dessert, he could eat no more.

Sister Raven peered through the window at the strange goings-on. She had to marvel at Coyote's clever trickery. But maybe, just maybe, she could outdo the Trickster with a trick of her own.

Davy wheeled his chair away from the table and toward the Christmas tree. "Santa," he asked, "can you stay long enough to open gifts with us?"

"Well, my boy," said Coyote, thinking about the bag full of worthless straw that he was about to leave as a gift, "I really should be going. I have many other visits to make on this special night."

Isabel pleaded, "Please stay just a little longer. Pleeease, Santa."

That's when the Trickster decided to make his getaway. He planned to jump from his chair, bound through the door, and be gone into the night. Instead, thanks to his full stomach, he stumbled off of his chair and fell headlong into the bag stuffed with straw. The sack burst open, spilling its contents upon the floor.

Coyote could not believe what he saw. Instead of straw, there were four big, wrapped packages tied with ribbon.

This unexpected magic was not his doing. Was it the work of some *Christmas* spirit? Thinking quickly, the rascal grabbed the package closest to him. The tag on it read, "Isabel." He gave it to the girl. Delightedly, she tore back the wrapping. It was a set of paints, brushes of all sizes, special drawing paper, and rows of colored pencils—just like the kind real artists use.

"Oh Santa, thank you!" she exclaimed. "I just love it."

Giving gifts was *not* the trick Coyote had intended. The
family opened their gifts in turn. Grandma got an entire set of
lovely china plates, bowls, cups, and saucers. Grandpa's gift
was a fleece-lined leather coat. Everyone was overjoyed. They
all looked on with smiling faces as Davy opened his Christmas
present. The boy sat in his wheelchair stunned and confused.
His package was empty. He turned to look for Coyote and
asked, "Santa?"

Coyote looked at Davy in his wheelchair and felt a twinge of guilt. The Trickster had never felt sorry for anyone before. This cruel trick was worse than he had planned. He headed for the door, and this time his legs carried him. He ran out into the snowy night. He climbed onto the top rail of the horse corral and turned to face everyone. Sister Raven watched the entire game from her perch atop a post. Brother Dog watched from his space under the porch. Even the horses in the barn looked out through the open door.

The family stood on the porch with surprised looks
upon their faces—looks that quickly turned to joy. For the
entire family stood, *even* Davy. His Christmas gift had not
been an empty package. It was in his *walking* legs. Davy
and his dog danced a little jig there in the snow. Everyone
waved good-bye and cheered, "Merry Christmas, Santa!"

Coyote pulled off his hat and waved it back and forth over his head. He did a fancy balancing act on the cross rail of the corral. With a gleeful smile he shouted, "Ho-ho-ho, merry Christmas!" Then his feet slipped apart. Down he went, doing the splits. He landed with a loud *thunk*, smack on the rail. It hurt! But Coyote grinned through his pain and managed to whimper one more "Ho-ho-ow!" as he hobbled off into the wintry night.

The horses were laughing up a storm. Poor Coyote had gotten his comeuppance. Sister Raven croaked a laugh, too. She had to wonder: Who had really been tricked this night? She spread her wings and hopped from her perch.

"Hey, Santa, you're walking kind of funny. Did you hurt yourself?" asked Sister Raven.

"No," lied the limping Coyote. He considered turning Sister Raven into a flying meatball. But he'd had enough meatballs and tricks for one night. Besides, it was Christmas Eve.

AUTHOR'S NOTE

When I was a boy, my mother told us children Coyote stories. They were traditional Native American tales that she had heard as a child growing up on the Standing Rock Indian Reservation in North Dakota, passed down by word of mouth from my Lakota/Sioux ancestors. My favorite stories, the ones that made me laugh out loud, were these fables about Coyote. They were humorous stories that taught a lesson, though they were also filled with danger and sometimes potent with the threat of being eaten—a child's worst fear! Although the stories were silly, often life and death hung in the balance.

Most people are familiar with the coyote. In the natural world, he is the four-legged animal that looks like a small wolf. He is also a mythological character with magical abilities. As such, Coyote is the infamous Trickster of Native American Indian legends. He is a loner and a wanderer. For countless generations he has lived among the Indian people of the American prairies. He has a reputation for being a clever liar, a sneaky thief, a womanizer, and a mischief-making clown. Coyote delights in playing pranks on animals and humans. When it comes to food, he will do anything for a free meal. Just when people think their lives are going along smoothly, you can count on Coyote to show up and play one of his dirty tricks. Quite often, he ends up getting caught in his own trick. Still, his antics teach a worthwhile lesson. Sometimes he actually ends up being the hero.

Coyote has many characteristics, mostly character flaws. He is greedy, needy, self-centered, and just downright wicked in a laughable way. It is his naughty behavior that sooner or later gets him in trouble. And that trouble usually comes with a comic twist. He never takes responsibility for his actions. Instead, he whines and blames others for his mistakes. It is his inappropriate behavior that teaches children a lesson—what *not* to do.

On a more fundamental level, Coyote's antics offer insights into an underlying dynamic of life itself—order and chaos. Coyote, of course, is the one who delivers chaos. When it comes to good and evil, Coyote is not the same as the Devil found in the Judeo-Christian tradition. Instead, Coyote reveals the paradoxical nature of life, capable of both good and evil. He reminds us that all of life is in a state of constant creation and destruction.

Coyote has the ability to transform himself. He can turn into a person, another animal, or even disappear. He can work magic—turn rags into clothing, cows into owls, and dogs into house cats.

Coyote Christmas is a contemporary story that takes place on the Standing Rock Indian Reservation in North Dakota. The times have changed—people no longer live in tipis, and horses have been replaced by cars and pickup trucks. There is even electricity for Christmas tree lights. However, one thing remains the same…Coyote is still up to his old tricks.

—S. D. Nelson

In a circle I am dancing
Snowflakes whirling round
Tiny tumbling snowflakes
Spinning to the ground

In stillness I am listening
Snowflakes murmur as they fall
Can you hear them whispering?
"Merry Christmas, one and all"
—S. D. Nelson

Artist's Note

The art for this book was created with
acrylic paint on 140-lb. cotton paper.

Library of Congress Cataloging-in-Publication Data:
Nelson, S. D.
Coyote Christmas / by S. D. Nelson.
p. cm.
Summary: His stomach rumbling, Coyote approaches a house on Christmas Eve hoping to trick the family there out of a hot meal by dressing as Santa Claus, but Sister Raven sees the strange events and plays a wonderful trick of her own.
ISBN-13: 978-0-8109-9367-9 (hardcover) / ISBN-10: 0-8109-9367-8 (hardcover)
1. Coyote (Legendary character)—Juvenile fiction. 2. Raven (Legendary character)—Juvenile fiction.
[1. Coyote (Legendary character)—Fiction. 2. Raven (Legendary character)—Fiction. 3. Tricksters—Fiction. 4. Christmas—Fiction. 5. Magic—Fiction.] I. Title.
PZ7.N4367Coy 2007
[E]—dc22
2006032614

Book design by Vivian Cheng

Printed and bound in China
10 9 8 7 6 5 4 3 2 1

HNA ▮▮▮▮▮
harry n. abrams, inc.
a subsidiary of La Martinière Groupe
115 West 18th Street
New York, NY 10011
www.hnabooks.com